SNIFFERS

Finds a Forever Home

By Sharon Row

Illustrations by Iwan Darmawan

SNIFFERS book series is dedicated to my grandson Logan Steadman. Together we created these stories about his cat Sniffers. We hope it brings awareness to adopt, rescue and help animals wherever and whenever possible.

copyright 2016 © Sharon Row All Rights Reserved

No part of Sniffers or any of its contents may be reproduced, copied, modified or adapted, without the prior written consent of the author for profit. Commercial use and distribution of the contents of the book is not allowed without express and prior written consent of the author.

SNIFFERS

Finds a Forever Home

By Sharon Row

Illustrations by Iwan Darmawan

There was a little boy named Logan. He asked his mom, "can I have a cat?"

His mom said, "do you know how to take care of a cat?"

"Yes mom. I'll make sure to love it, keep it warm, and I'll feed it every day."

After school, Logan and his mom drove to the rescue shelter. As Logan got out of the car he could hear lots of dogs barking. "Mom, why are those dogs barking?"

They're hoping someone will hear them and adopt them. A nice lady said, "Welcome to the rescue shelter. This is where sad cats and dogs come to stay until they find a forever home where someone will love them."

Slowly, the lady opened the door, and Logan's eye's got so big as he saw many cages filled with cats.

There were white cats, yellow cats, brown cats, black cats, and calico cats with mixes of different colors. Suddenly, Logan saw this one cage that had one black and white cat inside. Logan said, "That's the one I want!"

The mom turned to the lady and said, "Can my son get a closer look at this cat?" "This cat had a cold, but she's feeling much better now," the lady said.

Logan and his mom took a seat as the lady removed the cat from the cage.

Logan was surprised that the small cat jumped out of the lady's arms, and onto his lap. She was a little girl cat, and right away she started purring, stretching up to put her paws on Logan's shoulder's. Her whiskers tickled Logan's neck.

Logan said, "I will name Her Shiffers because she had a cold."

Shiffers couldn't believe what she was hearing. I finally get to leave this small wire cage with this lumpy, bumpy bed that makes me sheeze all the time.

Logan's mom went to a big pet store and filled a shopping cart with food, cat litter, toys, scratching pads, and a new soft pink bed.

Logan's mom said, "Logan, you better take Sniffers straight to your room. You don't want her to be scared on the first day in her new home."

Logan put her pink bed right next to his. Logan closed his eyes and said, "Good night, Sniffers, I love you." Sniffers was happy. Tonight, she would sleep in her new big room, and not in the cold wire cage at the shelter. I have my new home with the coolest, most fun kid. I bet he will help me hunt for mice and lizards.

Soon it was morning and the sun woke up Logan and Sniffers. After breakfast Logan got ready for school and told Sniffers, "I will see you as soon as school is out, and we can play togther."
But then Logan shut the door behind him.
Sniffers jumped up onto the window ledge to see what was going on.

Sniffers saw Logan and his mom drive away. Sniffers was so sad. She let out a big MEOW.
But wait, the window was open. Out jumped Sniffers and she started running faster and faster to catch the car.

After the car left Sniffers noticed the strangest thing. Something moved on the sidewalk. A small squirrel with a big rainbow-colored fluffy tail.

"Hi my name is Ginger," the squirrel said.

"Hi Ginger, my name is Sniffers. Do you know how to find Logan's school?" Ginger said, "I don't know, but I know someone who might. There's a dog named Sparkle, and she does not bite. She lives down the street by a green mailbox. Let's go look for her."

Soon they spotted the green mailbox. There was a pink dog that sparkled like glitter sitting in the sunlight.

"Hi Sparkle, do you know where I can find Logan's school?" said Sniffers.

"Let's go find Mayor Max," said Sparkle. "He always helps to do good deeds and give unconditional love to his friends, especially when it comes to helping rescue animals from the shelter. I'm sure he will help you Sniffers."

So Sparkle, Sniffers and Ginger went running down the street to find Mayor Max.

All of a sudden they slammed on their paw brakes because in the middle of the road was Mayor Max. He was so big. He was wearing a red tie with a special gold ribbon and blue medal around his neck. You just knew he was a very important dog.

Mayor Max said, "Hello Sniffers, Ginger and Sparkle. I do know where to find Logan's school. Meet my friend Mr. Peppalitas who can help you. He is a super hero cat who can fly."

"We need to hurry because any animal caught running around free will get taken to the animal shelter." said Mayor Max.
Sniffers didn't want to go back there, she just wanted to find Logan and feel safe again.

Suddenly, they all heard a van. "Quick follow me," Mayor Max said. But Sparkle was leaving glitter paw prints that anyone could follow. Mayor Max turned into an alley and said "Hide in here." There were large dirty garbage cans to hide behind.

Sniffers was sad and started to meow. "I don't think I will ever see Logan again." But out of the sky, something swooped down to pick up Sniffers. It was Mr. Peppalitas!

"Hello Sniffers, I will take you to Logan's school. Hold on tight." Mayor Max told Mr. Peppalitas, "Go fast! We'll be right behind you."
Up, Up, and away into the sky they went.

Sniffers wasn't afraid at all. She knew everything was safe while she was with Mr. Peppalitas.
Sniffers could see Logan's school as Mr. Peppalitas pointed down below with his paw.

The next thing Sniffers knew they were landing on the window ledge of Logan's classroom. Sniffers could see Logan sitting at his desk. She was so excited. Soon she will be with Logan again.

Mr. Peppalitas said to Sniffers, "I'm going to distract the teacher, and when I do, I want you to run over to Logan and hide in his desk." Sniffers was so excited to see Logan. Mr. Peppalitas started flying around in circles inside the classroom.

The teacher's eyes went wide, her mouth a big round O. Nobody's ever seen a superhero flying cat before.

While the teacher was busy chasing Mr. Peppalitas, Sniffers jumped into the classroom.

Sniffers ran straight to Logan's desk to hide. Logan and all the kids were so busy watching Mr. Peppalitas that they didn't notice Sniffers sneak in. Sniffers looked up, and Mr. Peppalitas gave her a big wink before fying out the window.

The teacher ran to the window and rubbed her eyes. "Was that really a superhero flying cat?" she asked the class.

Sniffers purred, and when Logan looked down, he was so surprised to see Sniffers. Her little black and white head was looking up at him.

Logan opened his backpack, and Sniffers jumped inside. He zipped it closed, leaving just enough room for Sniffers to breathe.

Just then the school bell rang and it was time to go.

Logan got his backpack and ran out the door to the car where his mom was waiting.

He got in and put his backpack on his lap. His mom said, "How was your day, Logan?" Logan could hardly breathe as he told his mom about the amazing flying superhero cat and how, like magic, Sniffers appears in his desk.

Logan slowly unzipped the backpack and Sniffers head popped out. Logan's mom was so surprised. She listened to Logan's story and said, "Wow Logan, you sure adopted a incrediable cat to have many special adventures with."

Thank you for reading SNIFFERS and always remember to keep your pets spayed and neutered. The best forever friends with unconditional love are just waiting for you. Find them at your local rescue shelters.

LOGAN
AND
SNIFFERS

MAYOR MAX

Mayor of Idyllwild, California

www.mayormax.com

Mayor Max is the official Mayor of Idyllwild, CA. He is a role model for giving unconditional love to everyone he meets.

Made in the
USA
Lexington, KY

54228473R00031